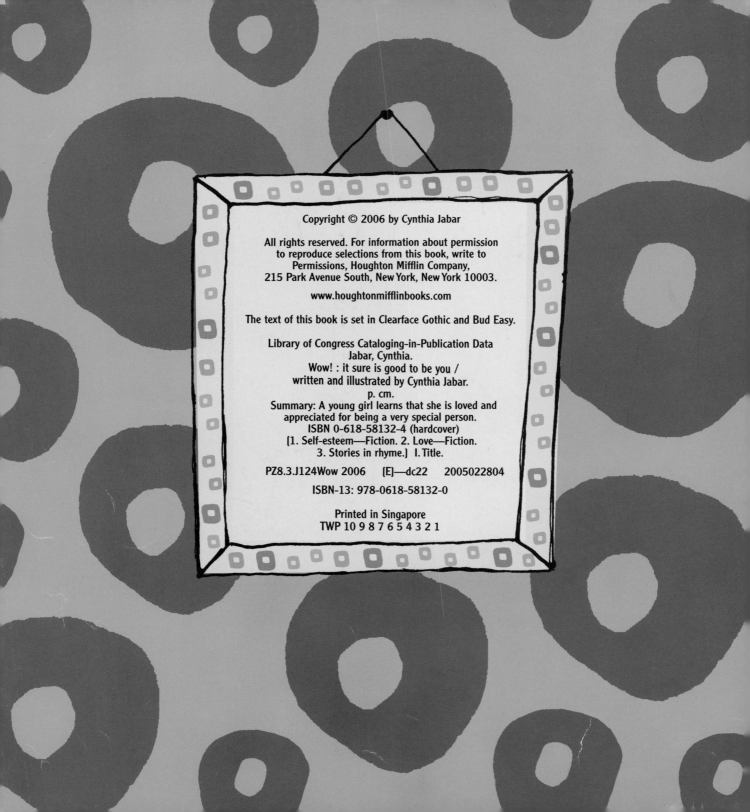

www.houghtonmifflinbooks.com

The text of this book is set in Clearface Gothic and Bud Easy.

Library of Congress Cataloging-in-Publication Data
Jabar, Cynthia.
Wow! : it sure is good to be you /
written and illustrated by Cynthia Jabar.
p. cm.
Summary: A young girl learns that she is loved and
appreciated for being a very special person.
ISBN 0-618-58132-4 (hardcover)
[1. Self-esteem—Fiction. 2. Love—Fiction.
3. Stories in rhyme.] I. Title.

PZ8.3.J124Wow 2006   [E]—dc22   2005022804

ISBN-13: 978-0618-58132-0

Printed in Singapore
TWP 10 9 8 7 6 5 4 3 2 1

WOW!
It Sure Is Good To Be You!

Written and illustrated by Cynthia Jabar

Houghton Mifflin Company
Boston 2006

Somebody, somewhere,
is thinking about you,

Keeps your picture in their pocket,

Misses your kisses,

Loves you more than birds love trees,
more than brothers love to tease,
loves you even more than dogs have fleas,
and that's a lot, too!

Loving you is their favorite thing to do.

WOW!

It sure is good to be you!

Somebody, somewhere,
remembers your silly faces,
and sad ones, too,
wishes you all the luck in the universe,

Is always
very proud of you!

Somebody, somewhere,
is missing you, too,

Loves you no matter what you say or do,

Loves you
toe-tap-happy
loud,

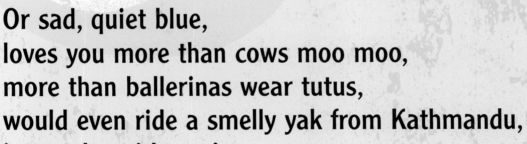

Or sad, quiet blue,
loves you more than cows moo moo,
more than ballerinas wear tutus,
would even ride a smelly yak from Kathmandu,
just to be with you!
And that's really far, too!

WOW!

It sure is good to be you!

Somebody, somewhere, knows you're cool-girl brave and strong,

With amazing talents.
Why, even your short list
goes on and on and on . . .

YOU ROCK!

Brave
nice to cats
smart
math wiz
cool
loyal
friend
fun
artist

And now,
somebody, somewhere,
is coming to visit,
to love you and laugh,
and share some special time.

Because now is the gift,
and now you're all mine!

I'll love you forever plus always,
and that's really long, too!

WOW!

It sure is good to be you!